Beasties

by Pat Hall
illustrated by Emmeline Hall Forrestal

To Michael —
Enjoy!
Pat Hall
2018

Beasties

by Pat Hall

illustrated by Emmeline Hall Forrestal

Crow's Foot Books
Minnesota • Wisconsin

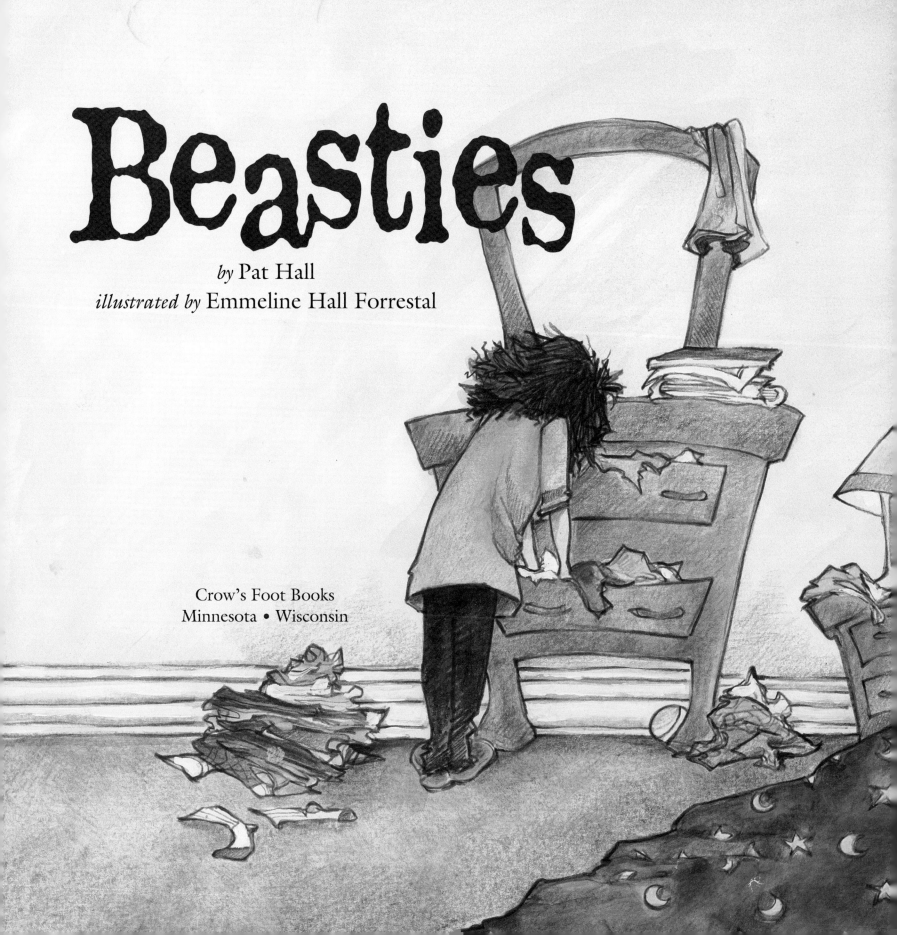

Crow's Foot Books
419 Williams Street
Janesville, WI 53545

crowsfootbooks@gmail.com
www.emmelineforrestal.com

Printed and bound in the United States of America
First Edition
10 9 8 7 6 5 4 3 2 1
LCCN on file
ISBN 978-0-692-49693-0

book bridge press

This book was expertly produced by Book Bridge Press
www.bookbridgepress.com

Many thanks go to my son Matthew for using his analytical skills
in the development of the cookie recipe.
Son Michael nobly forced himself to evaluate many variations.
Daughter Christina and I had fun and valuable discussions
on rhythms and word choices.
Daughter Emmeline has brought the story
to life with her illustrations.
Husband Tom is always a source of love and encouragement.
Aimee, Lois, Helga, and the staff of Book Bridge Press were a joy
to work with, and I thank them for their expertise.
Thanks also to friends and family who test-drove the recipe.

I became aware of the superstition of warding off werewolves
and vampires with counting tasks from the book, *Sand: A Journey
Through Science and the Imagination* by Michael Welland.

—P. H.

For Spike, of course

—E. H. F.

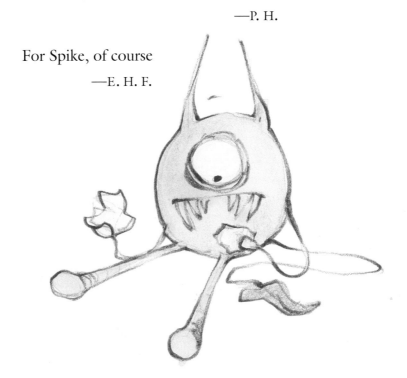

"**T**he world is full of beasties, dear," my granny always said.

"They might be LARGE and LUNGE about,

or SMALL and CREEP instead.

They could be covered up with fur, or scales an icky green,

but here's the thing you need to know if beasties might be seen.

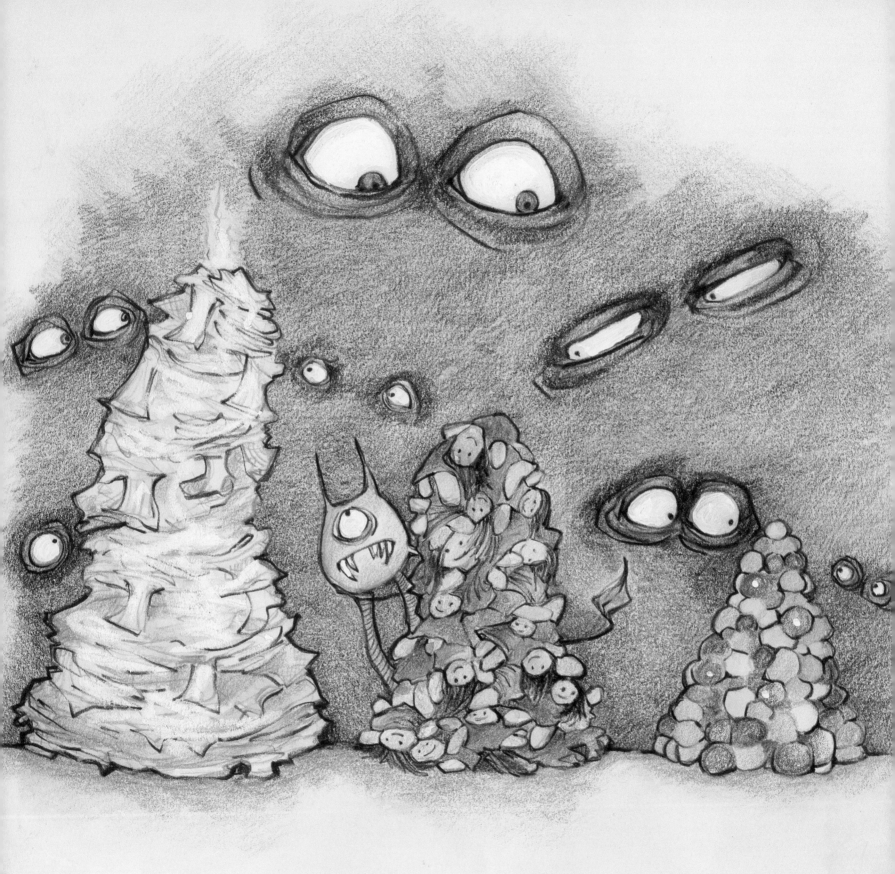

Should beasties spy a group of things all similar in size,

their FINGERS ITCH to add them up.
They can't avert THEIR EYES.

If you can get them counting—here's a fact both tried and true—

however high the number, they won't stop until they're through."

Thanks to Granny's warning, there's a sieve beneath my bed.

Beasties there can't scare me 'cause they have to count instead.

With NASTY little CLAWS
and FANGS
and BULGY little EYES,

they number each and every hole with angry little sighs.

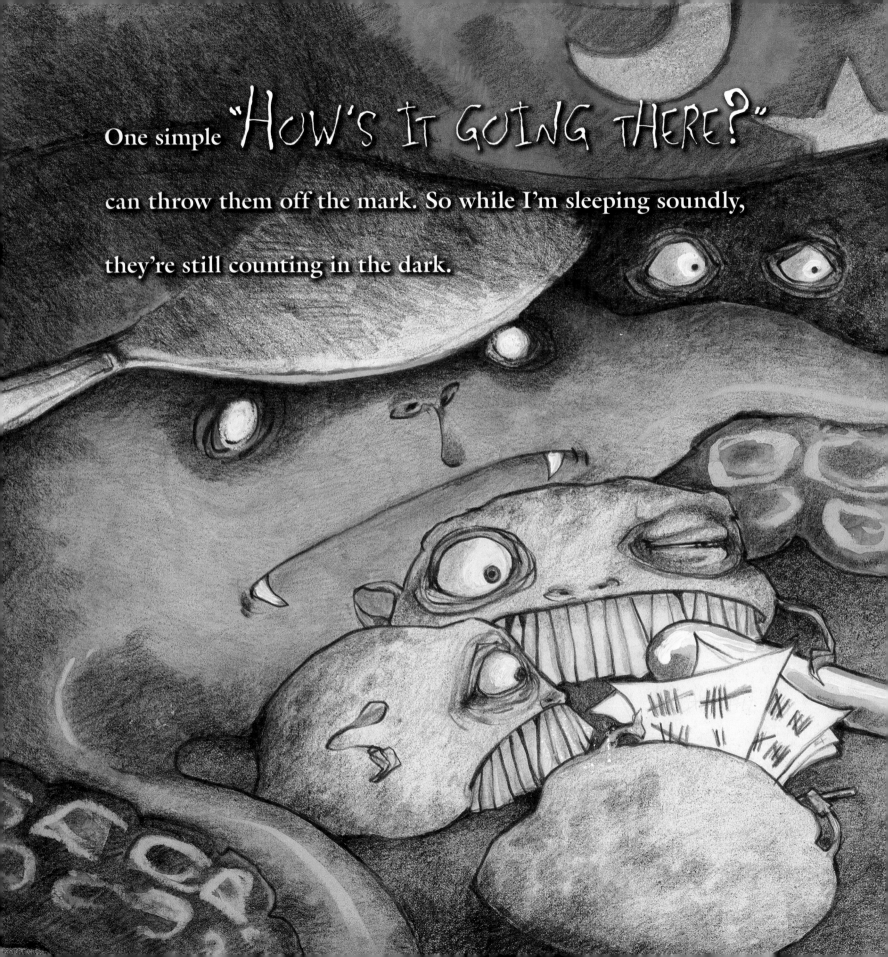

One simple "HOW'S IT GOING THERE?" can throw them off the mark. So while I'm sleeping soundly, they're still counting in the dark.

Time again and time again, my granny took my hand,

warning, "Never take a walk without a handy bag of sand."

If I'm BEING FOLLOWED by a WOLFISH, TOOTHY GROUP,

I reach inside my pocket for my sandy little scoop.

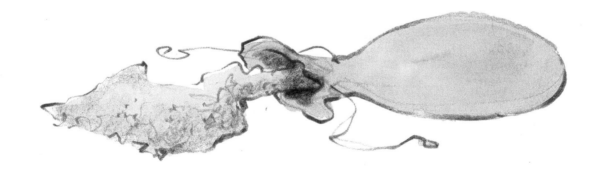

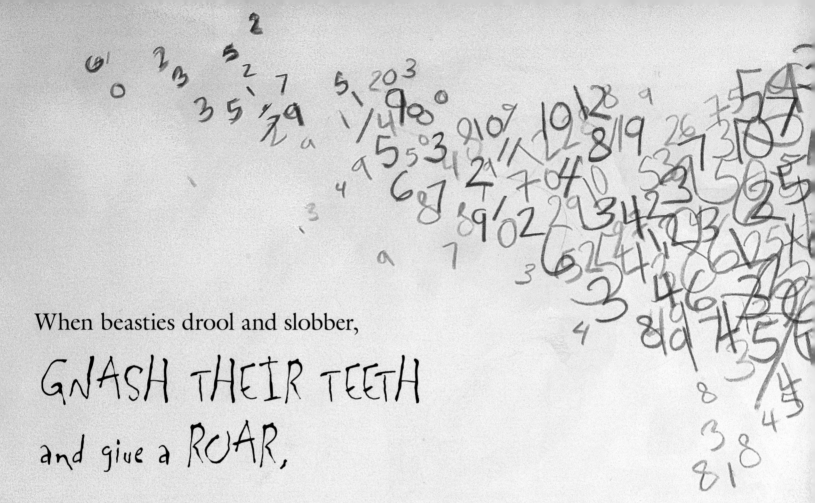

When beasties drool and slobber,

GNASH THEIR TEETH
and give a ROAR,

"Hey, wait!" I say. "Look here!" I show the bag and start to pour.

Oh! They can't resist the challenge! Numbers burn inside their brains!

As I run off to safety, they sit counting tiny grains.

No matter what I'm doing,

if I feel a BEASTIE STARE,

I spread my things around me in a circle everywhere.

In Granny's words, "It looks a mess, but we know what it's for.

It SCARES AWAY the BEASTIES

with another counting chore."

As I know my granny did, I really like the rain.

The soothing sound of water drops erases any pain.

But rainy pitter-patter puts the

BEASTIES in a TIZZY.

They frantically count raindrops till they're

FALLING DOWN and DIZZY.

While I am baking cookies, cozy, warm and trouble-free,

the beasts are getting soggy and as crabby as can be.

They spit! They whine! They're doubly cross, because they realize

they've got to count the raindrops

and their

DRIPPING HAIRS besides.

"Let's call a truce," I say to them. "Come in and dry your hair.

I've been baking cookies like my granny used to share."

"Oh, no!" the tearful beasties cry,

with QUIVERS in their LIPS,

"We can't have any cookies till we count the chocolate chips!"

"Then just this once I'll tell you, but no scaring past this door!

The chocolate chips add up to be six hundred thirty-four!"

"That's CLOSE ENOUGH!" the beasties cry.

"We're HAPPY with your NUMBER.

May we have some cookies and curl up here for a slumber?"

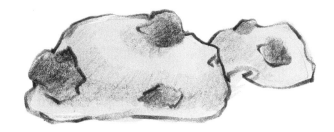

The secret is, the counting wasn't really done by me.

The number was already there in Granny's recipe.

Because as Granny also told me, "Listen, don't forget,

a BEASTIE might turn out to be a FRIEND you HAVEN'T MET."

Beastly-Good Cookies

Ingredients:

1 cup butter (2 sticks), browned*

2 cups brown sugar

6 tablespoons milk

1½ teaspoons salt

1 teaspoon vanilla extract

2 eggs

3 cups flour

1¼ teaspoons baking soda

634 chocolate chips (one 12-ounce bag)

Directions:

To make these cookies you have to use the stove and the oven and lift things that will be very hot! Please ask an adult to help you.

1. Pour the browned butter into a large bowl. Careful! It will be hot! Stir in the brown sugar and the milk. Add the salt, the vanilla, and the eggs. Stir well.

2. In a separate bowl, stir together the flour and the baking soda. Add this mixture to the butter in the large bowl and stir. Stir in the chocolate chips.

3. Chill the dough in the refrigerator for 60 minutes. Preheat the oven to 375 degrees.

4. Drop the chilled dough by rounded tablespoons onto an ungreased cookie sheet. Bake for 9 to 11 minutes, or until lightly browned. Don't over bake. Cool on a rack.

   Makes 53 cookies.

* *The browning process takes about 5 to 6 minutes. It's best to use a light-colored pan so you can see the color change.*

Put the butter in the pan and cook over medium heat on the stove, stirring constantly. The butter will melt and start to foam, then stop foaming and come to a boil. Watch carefully and keep stirring for a few minutes. As soon as the butter starts to turn golden brown, pour it into the large bowl to stop the cooking. Go ahead with the rest of the recipe. The butter doesn't need to cool beforehand.

PAT HALL counts her favorite things as family, writing, gardening, volunteering, community theater, and making Ukrainian-style decorated eggs. Her award-winning book, *Ida May's Borrowed Trouble*, was also illustrated by Emmeline.

EMMELINE HALL FORRESTAL is the award-winning illustrator of four books for children. She lives with her family in Minnesota. You can see more of her work at www.emmelineforrestal.com, or follow her on Twitter @boredcelery.